Sexy Adultery Erotica

I0547749

She's A Big Girl Now

Just Plain Bob

WARNING

This book contains sexually explicit scenes and adult language. It may be considered offensive to some readers. This book is for sale to adults ONLY.

Please store your files wisely where they cannot be accessed by underage readers.

* * * * * * * * * * * * * * * * * * * *

WANT FREE COPIES OF MY BOOKS?

Just visit my blog and download free copies of my books:

awesomeauthors.org/justplainbob

About the Publisher

4Fun Publishing, a member of **BLVNP Incorporated**, 340 S. Lemon #6200, Walnut CA 91789, info@blvnp.com / legal@blvnp.com
NOTE: Due to the highly emotional reaction of some people to works of erotic fiction, any email sent to the above address that contains foul language or religious references is automatically deleted by our anti-spam software and will not be seen. All other communications are welcome.

DISCLAIMER

Please don't be stupid and kill yourself. This book is a work of FICTION. Do not try any new sexual practice that you find in this book. It is fiction and not to be confused with reality. Neither the author nor the publisher or its associates assume any responsibility for any loss, injury, death or legal consequences resulting from acting on the contents in this book. Every character in this book is over 18 years of age. The author's opinions are not to be construed as the opinions of the publisher. The material in this book is for entertainment purposes ONLY. Enjoy.

She's A Big Girl Now

Sexy Adultery Erotica

By: Just Plain Bob

© Just Plain Bob 2015
ISBN: 978-1-68030-530-2

I should have known disaster was on the horizon the night my wife told me that she'd had a call from Monica. It was at the dinner table and my first tip off should have been the fact that everything on the table was from my list of favorites. Meat loaf, scalloped potatoes au gratin, French style green beans and sourdough bread hot from the oven. Midway through the meal Audrey said:

"Guess who I heard from today. Monica Speers. She moved back to town and wants to get together for lunch."

"Moved back to town? XYZ doesn't have offices here. Did Tom quit them?"

"I guess she and Tom are divorced."

I knew what I wanted to say to that and I knew that it would not go over well so I kept my mouth shut. I would have bet that it was because Tom finally caught her cheating. I did not like Monica and I had never liked Audrey associating with her, but if there was one thing I knew it was that there was no way you could come between two girls who had been best friends since the second grade.

***

I didn't meet Audrey and Monica until high school and it was a case of 'instants.' I instantly fell ass end over tea kettle for Audrey and I instantly disliked Monica. There was just something about her that did not ring right.

I would like to be able to say that Audrey was as instantly attracted to me as I was to her, but that wasn't the case. I tried a dozen times to get Audrey to go out with me but with no luck and I always felt that it was because of Monica. Monica hit the ground running when she started high school. She was a hot looking freshman who looked like she was twenty and the juniors and seniors flocked to her and as a result she was dating them from almost her first day. It always seemed that the guy she was dating had a friend he wanted to double date with so Monica would set up the friend with Audrey.

By the tenth grade Monica had a reputation as a 'wild child' who could be counted on to give it up by the third date. Audrey also had a reputation. She was known as "The Ice Queen." She would neck, but she wouldn't put out. I heard about double dates where she and Monica would end up in a bedroom and Monica would strap on her date while Audrey sat on the edge of the bed and swapped tongues with hers (I never had the nerve to ask Audrey if there was any truth to the stories). I'd even heard (and Bud Wilson swears that it is true) that when Monica had finished draining her date, she would take on Audrey's date. So what I got whenever I asked Audrey out was:

"Sorry Rob, but I already have a date for that night."

Eventually I added Audrey to the list of things I wanted, but could never have.

Two weeks after the start of the eleventh grade I was sitting in a booth at Harry's Malt Shop- a student hangout, when someone slid into the booth opposite me. I looked up from the Civics text book I was reading and saw Audrey. She smiled and said:

"Hi Rob."

"Hello Audrey."

"How have you been?"

"Okay. You?"

"Pretty good. I see you are studying Civics. Who do you have?"

"Anderson in second period."

"I've got her in fifth."

She was silent for a second or two and then said, "It has been a while since I've seen you."

"Well you know how it is. You get busy and things kind of slide."

A little more silence and then, "There is a party at Nancy Neubert's this Friday. Would you like to go with me?"

That caught me flat-footed. I had tried for two years to get a date with her with no luck at all and here she was asking me. It took me a couple of seconds to come up with a reply.

"I haven't been invited."

"I have and I can bring a date. Would you like to go?"

"Yes, I would."

"Okay then, meet me tomorrow at lunch in the cafeteria and we can discuss the details."

"Details?"

"What time to pick me up, where we are going and things like that."

"Oh sure, details. Right."

As she walked away I sat and wondered just what the hell had happened. And then it dawned on me. All the juniors and seniors that Monica and Audrey had been dating had graduated and had moved on to college where there were plenty of girls and they didn't need to mess around with high school girls any more. That meant that if Audrey and Monica wanted dates they were stuck with their previously ignored classmates. Whatever the reason, I wasn't going to complain.

My mother let me borrow her car on Friday and I drove over and picked up Audrey. When we got to Nancy's, we found that the party was spread all through the house. The garage had been cleared out so there would be a place to dance and the Neuberts had turned their basement into a rec room with a pool table, a ping-pong table and an air hockey table.

When Audrey and I went into the garage, the first person we saw was Monica. She was with four guys at the back of the garage where there was a table with a reel to reel tape player on it. The tape was playing dance tunes and Monica saw us just about the time we saw her. She came over to us and said to Audrey:

"Glad you could make it."

Audrey asked me if I would find out where the refreshments were and get her a Coke or a Pepsi and that is where I made my first mistake. I should have kept her with me. I found the refreshments in the kitchen and by the time I got back to the garage Audrey was dancing with one of the guys who had been with Monica when we arrived. Because my parents had taken the time to teach me manners I stood off to the side and waited for the song to end and that was my second mistake.

As soon as the song ended the next song on the reel began to play and another one of the guys who had been talking with Monica stepped up and started dancing with Audrey. I saw Audrey see me standing there with a Pepsi in my hand for her, but she didn't pull away from the guy and come to me. About half way into the dance Monica came over to me and reached out for the Pepsi I was holding for Audrey and said:

"I'll take that. You might as well find something else to do. She's going to be busy for a while."

While she was saying that, the music stopped. I started toward Audrey and she was standing there looking at me walking toward her when the next song started. A third guy took her arm and she let him start dancing with her. She saw me walking towards her with the soft drink she had asked me to get for her and she let herself be pulled into a dance and then to add insult to injury, she never looked my way again.

I let Monica take the Pepsi and I walked over and tapped the guy on the shoulder and said:

"Cutting in."

"Screw off jerk."

"She is my date and I'm cutting in."

"Beat it asswipe," the guy said and he reached out with his left hand to push me away. When he pushed at me I grabbed his hand and jerked. It pulled him off balance and I just kept pulling until I ran him into the wall. His head bounced against the wall and it stunned him and he slid down to the floor. While all that was going on Audrey was saying:

"Stop this Rob, stop this now. You are embarrassing me."

I looked at her and said, "I'm embarrassing you? Well, we sure wouldn't want that." I left the garage, got in my car and went home.

Monday morning I was at my locker getting ready to go to first period when Nancy Neubert came up to me and said:

"I should be pissed at you for creating a disturbance at my party, but I'm not. Doug is a real butt head and I'm glad someone stepped up and shut him down."

"Sorry. It was poor manners on my part."

"You don't need to apologize. Doug wasn't even invited but your date was a little pissed that you went off and left her."

"She left me first. It seems she was more interested in the guys Monica was with than me."

"Aud would be okay if she could just break away from Monica."

"Maybe I'll have better luck next time."

"Good luck," she said as she moved off to her first class.

I didn't have any shared morning classes with Audrey so I didn't expect to see her until our one o'clock calculus class. I guess it shouldn't have been a surprise (given that Nancy had already told me how upset Audrey was that I'd gone off and left her) that she sat down across from me in the cafeteria at lunch time. I looked up at her and she sat there and said nothing so I went back to eating my lunch and reviewing my notes from Civics. After maybe a minute Audrey said:

"Are you just going to sit there?"

"What do you expect me to do, dance?"

"I expect you to tell me why you acted like a total ass and then I expect an apology for the way you behaved toward me."

"You expect to live to be a hundred?"

"What?"

"Easy question Audrey; do you expect to live to be a hundred? Because it will be your hundredth birthday before you get an apology from me for what your behavior caused me to do last Friday."

"My behavior? Are you out of your mind?"

"No, but you must have been if you thought that I would put up with what you did."

"What I did?"

"Yes Audrey, what you did. We no sooner got to the party and you sent me off to get you a Coke and then you busied yourself with all the guys who were hanging with Monica when we got there. You even sent Monica over to tell me to take a hike."

"I never did that!"

"You deny sending Monica over to tell me to bug off?"

"She would never do something like that."

"The hell she wouldn't. I came back with a Pepsi for you and she came over to me and said she would take it and hold it for you. Her exact words were "You might as well find something else to do. She's going to be busy for a while." When she said that, I tried to cut in and remind you whose date you were and the asshole you were dancing with got mouthy and tried to get physical and when I got physical back you told me that I was embarrassing you. That was a laugh. Me embarrassing you? How about the embarrassment you caused me? How do you think it looked to everyone there when as soon as we get to the party my date abandons me for a bunch of Monica's assholes? It will be a cold day in hell before you get an apology out of me. Now if you don't mind I'd like to finish my lunch." Then I went back to eating.

She sat there silent, watching me for maybe a minute then she got up and left.

I saw her again in the two afternoon classes we shared and she ignored me, which didn't bother me at all.

Three weeks went by and then one Thursday I was again sitting in Harry's Malt Shop when Audrey sat down across from me. I looked up from the notes I was reviewing, saw that it was Audrey and went back to my notes. Maybe a minute passed and then Audrey said:

"I'm here to eat crow Rob." I looked up at her and she said, "You were right. My behavior was uncalled for and I can't offer any good excuse for it other than I was asked to dance and you weren't back yet so I said yes and then things got out of hand. After talking with you in the cafeteria and thinking about it I was all set to apologize until I asked Monica why she said what you said she said. She denied it and said you were lying to cover up for being an asshole so I stopped thinking about apologizing. It wasn't until last Sunday that I found out that it was Monica who lied. Gail Luoma told me that she heard Monica say it to you. It has taken me until now to work up the courage to face you. I'm sorry Rob. Can we get by this and maybe try again?"

I looked at her for several seconds and then said, "What do you have in mind when you say "try again"?"

"Well, since our first date didn't go too well I thought maybe we could give it another try?"

"You have anything planned for Saturday?"

"No."

"Would you like to go to the movies with me?"

"I'd love to."

The date went well and it led to a second one which in turn led to a third and suddenly Audrey and I were a couple. The only fly in the ointment was that Audrey sometimes had us double dating with Monica and her butt-head of the moment. I say that because Monica seemed incapable of dating a guy who wasn't an obnoxious asshole. On many a date it was all I could do to keep my mouth shut and not create a scene. What amazed me was that Audrey never seemed to notice or care.

Things were good between Audrey and me until two weeks before senior prom. Audrey and I had a date to attend a concert on Sunday and Saturday evening she called me and told me that she had to cancel because of a family emergency. Those things happen and so I thought nothing about it. I didn't feel like going to the concert alone so I called a couple of guys I knew and we went over to check out a new arcade that had opened on the west side of town.

The first thing I saw when I walked into the arcade was Audrey, Monica and two guys standing in line to buy game tokens. I debated going over to her and saying something about 'family emergencies' but decided against it. She would see me sooner or later and know that I'd seen her. Hopefully the knowledge that she was busted would ruin her night. Actually it would do more than ruin her night. It would cast a pall on some other things also. For one, although she didn't know it yet, she was going to need a date for the prom since she damned sure wouldn't be going with me.

I happened to be looking at her reflection in the glass panel on the back of the pin ball machine I was playing when she saw me. Her hand flew up to her mouth and she hurriedly turned away, said something to Monica and then she, Monica and the two guys split and I didn't see them again that night

Audrey wasn't in school Monday and I didn't call her. Tuesday Audrey walked up to the table I was sitting at during lunch period and sat down. She said:

"Can we talk Rob?"

I said no and got up and walked away. She tried to get me to talk to her following both afternoon classes and I simply walked by her without saying a word. Wednesday she again approached me in the cafeteria.

"We need to talk Rob."

"About what?"

"About what we are going to be doing on prom night."

"I have no idea what you will be doing. I'll be going stag."

Her face went pale and she said, "You aren't taking me?"

"No Audrey, I'm not. You can go with the guy you went out with Sunday night. Or maybe you can give your good friend Monica a call. She always seems to be able to come up with dates for you."

I got up and walked away leaving her sitting there with tears running down her face.

Saturday Harlina Collins called me at home. After some small talk she said:

"Something happen between you and Audrey?"

"You could say that. Why?"

"She is running around frantically trying to find a date for the prom. I take it that she isn't going with you?"

"No she isn't."

"Who are you taking?"

"No one. I'll be going stag."

"Would you like a date?"

"It is a little late to be looking for a date. By now everyone will be spoken for."

"Not necessarily. I need a date."

"You? What happened between you and Toby?"

"Nothing happened between us. Yesterday he went to the hospital with a burst appendix and he is going to be off his feet for at least two weeks. No way he can make it to the prom next Friday."

"Will you going with me create problems between the two of you?"

"No. I already asked Toby and he said he was okay with it."

"Then you have a date."

Harlina and I had a great time at the prom and at the two after prom parties we attended. I do have to say that the kiss she gave me when I took her home would not have passed the 'boyfriend test' but other than that we behaved ourselves.

Audrey did manage to come up with a date or more likely Monica found her one since the guy wasn't someone who went to our school. Audrey did not seem like she was having all that good of a time, but hey! Not my problem.

Audrey and I pretty much steered clear of each other for the rest of our senior year. Me because she had lied to me and did what I considered as stabbing me in the back and her because, as I heard through the grapevine, she blamed me for ruining her senior prom.

Graduation came and my parents gave me a three year old Mustang convertible as a graduation present and that made my summer dating much easier. I dated a lot, but I never hooked up with anyone steady. I spent the summer working for the landscape company I had worked for the previous two summers and then in the fall I was off to college.

As fate would have it, Audrey and I were thrown together on our first day of classes. We were both Business Management majors and had four shared classes. We avoided each other for most of the first term, but then in Introduction to Production Management the instructor split the class up into eight groups of four students each and assigned group projects. I ended up in the same group as Audrey. There was no way around it, we had to socialize because we had to research together and work together with the other two in the group in order to complete the project.

One afternoon when all four of us were supposed to meet at the library I got there first and was sitting at a table in the reference section when Audrey showed up. She sat down and we pretty much ignored each other for a couple of minutes before Audrey said:

"This is just stupid. We are supposed to be adults now so why are we acting like children. We have known each other for years so we should be able to talk to each other. How have you been Rob?"

"Not bad Audrey. You?"

"I've been better. I could have done without being put on this project with you."

"Sorry you have to put up with me, but it wasn't my choice."

"It's not the putting up with you Rob, it is the being around you and knowing that you don't like me."

Before I could say anything the other two showed up and we got busy on the project. When the group broke up I asked Audrey if she would like to have a cup of coffee with me. She hesitated slightly before saying that she would like to and I told her I would meet her at the student union in ten minutes and then I went over to the check-out desk and checked out a couple of books.

Audrey was sitting at a table when I got to the cafeteria and I joined her after getting a cup of coffee and a piece of pie. As I sat down I said:

"Where did you get the idea that I don't like you?"

"From the way you dumped me just before the prom and then would never talk to me after."

"That had nothing to do with me liking you Audrey. Do you honestly expect me to believe that you don't know why it happened?"

"I didn't do anything to deserve that Rob."

"In my mind you did. You broke a date with me so you could go out with another guy."

"But I didn't do it because I liked the other guy. I only did it because Monica needed me to help her out. She wanted to go out with this guy, but he had a friend visiting and he couldn't go off and leave him alone so Monica asked me to double with her. The guy meant nothing to me. It was just one date and I never saw him again."

"Then that is what you should have told me instead of lying to me about a family emergency. You should have been up front with me. I wouldn't have liked it and it would have probably pissed me off, but I would have gotten over it, but to catch you in a lie? No way could I accept that."

"I guess you are right. I shouldn't have lied, but I knew you didn't care for Monica so I didn't want to bring her into it. I thought I could do it and you would never know so things would be okay. I'm sorry Rob, I really am sorry."

I said nothing and she was silent for maybe twenty seconds and then she said:

"I've missed you Rob."

"I've missed you too Audrey."

"Can we get back to being friends?"

"I don't see why not."

From that point on we were back to talking, although I made no attempt to ask her out. For one thing I'd already been burned twice by her, with Monica's help, and Monica was still around. I did date though and at various parties and other activities I'd see Monica, Audrey and the guys they were with. I never did seem to see Monica or Audrey with the same guy twice in a row.

Audrey and I lunched together often in the cafeteria and since we shared many of the same classes we met after class at the library to study. During one of those study sessions Audrey asked:

"Are we ever going to get back to the way we were?"

"What do you mean?"

"Are you ever going to ask me out again?"

"I don't know Audrey. To be honest about it I was pretty much stuck on you, but twice you burned me because of Monica and you still run with her. I don't feel much like setting myself up to get dumped on again."

"Do you really think I would do that to you?"

"You already have Audrey, twice."

"I was younger and a little more flighty then Rob. I have grown up a lot."

I took a chance and asked for a date and, as the last time, one led to two which led to a third and then we were keeping each other company again. On our fifth date we made love for the first time. There previously had been a lot of hot and heavy necking, but we had never gone all the way. Neither of us were virgins and though I knew it was unreasonable of me I was really pissed that Audrey wasn't. Mostly because she had probably lost it to one of the guys Monica was always setting her up with instead of me. However we seemed to fit well together and after that first time we made love three or four times a week.

As it had been before a lot of our dates were double dates with Monica and her taste in guys hadn't improved any, but also as before I kept my mouth shut and bore up under it as best I could.

We made it through our freshman and sophomore years without any more problems and I was beginning to think of our future after graduation. I was even to the point of stopping and looking in jewelry store windows at rings. One month into our senior year the Monica Monster raised its ugly head again.

It was a Thursday and we were having lunch at the cafeteria in the student union and Audrey asked:

"We don't have anything going this Saturday do we?"

"Not that I can think of. Why?"

"Monica wants me to do her a favor."

"What kind of favor?"

"This guy she is seeing has a friend coming to town for the weekend."

"Are you the only girl that Monica knows? Why is it always you that has to be the one that she sets up with her boyfriend's friends?"

"I'm sure that she knows other girls, but I'm her best friend and she just feels more comfortable when it is me with her."

"Well I'm not comfortable with it. I thought we had something working for us Aud, but you going off and dating other guys makes me wonder."

"Don't be that way Rob. It doesn't mean a thing. We will go to dinner and maybe a movie. Probably stop for a drink or two and some dancing and then I'll go home. It is just a favor to Monica and you just said that we don't have anything planned. It will be okay."

"I don't own you Audrey, but I'm going to say that I don't like it. I'm not happy with it at all." I got up and walked away from the table.

I had hoped the way I left would give her pause and make her rethink things. I didn't see her again until lunch the next day. We talked about classes and things and after I finished eating I said:

"You want to do something this weekend?"

"Did you forget I'm going out with Monica?"

"No, but I had hoped that you would have thought it over and decided not to do it."

"We doing anything tonight?"

"I don't know about you, but I'm going to call around and see if anybody has a sister or a female cousin or female friend coming to town who needs a date." I got up and left her sitting there.

She tried to talk to me after our afternoon class, but I didn't stop to talk. She called me twice that night. The first time she told me that I was being unreasonable and I told her not to my way of thinking and I hung up on her. The second time she gave me a ration of shit for hanging up on her and I hung up on her again.

Saturday I called around and found a couple of guys to go out drinking with. Mike had heard of a new place out on the turnpike and so we went out that way to check the place out. We had been there maybe an hour when Ben said:

"Isn't that Audrey?"

I looked and sure enough it was Audrey, Monica and two guys. One guy had his arm around Audrey and she was looking up at him and smiling. They took a table at the other end of the room from us and ordered drinks. The guy who had his arm around Audrey leaned over and said something to her and she laughed and then they kissed. They got up to dance and moved so close together that I doubt you would have been able to slide a sheet of paper between them. Audrey had both arms around his neck and he had both hands on her ass pulling her into him.

I watched for an hour as they danced and kissed and then I'd had enough. I told Ben and Mike that I needed to move to some other place to do my drinking or I would probably end up in jail for creating a very nasty disturbance. We got up to leave and I stopped at Audrey's table. When she saw me I saw her face change to an "Oh shit!" look and I leaned down and said to Audrey's guy:

"She is a great piece of ass, but make sure that you use a condom. The last time I fucked her she gave me a bad case of cock rot. Took damned near a month to clear up."

Then I looked Audrey in the eye and said, "Nice seeing you again Aud," Then I walked away.

Mike, Ben and I went over to the Landing Strip Lounge near the airport and saw Harlina Collins, Nancy Neubert and Bev Holbrook sitting at a table and they waved us over to join them. We danced and drank with the girls until closing and then hit the Denny's on Wayne Road for an early breakfast. Harlina was riding with Bev and as we finished eating Harlina commented on the fact that she lived close to me and could I give her a ride home since Bev lived in the opposite direction so I told her no problem. Bev took Mike with her since they only lived two blocks apart. Ben and Nancy had been making eyes at each other all night so they left together.

Once in my car I asked Harlina why she wasn't out with Toby on a Saturday night.

"Toby is history."

"Oh? When did that happen?"

"When I caught him screwing Helen Liss."

"I didn't know. Sorry."

"I'm not. Better to find out he is a cheating asshole now rather than later. Why aren't you with Audrey tonight?"

"Pretty much for the same reason you aren't with Toby."

"We can sure pick them."

I didn't say anything to that and after maybe a minute Harlina looked over at me and said:

"You know what I'm the most sorry about?"

"No idea."

"I was so looking forward to giving up my cherry on prom night, but then Toby ended up in the hospital. I almost talked myself into letting you do the deed, but at the last minute I decided to stay true to Toby. Too bad that I didn't know then what I know now." She was silent for a bit and then she said, "Any interest in seeing what we both missed out on?"

After what I'd seen Audrey doing, I owed her nothing so I looked over at Harlina and smiled.

The hot kiss that Harlina had given me on prom night had hinted at the passion inside her waiting to be released. If what she gave me was even half of what she'd had inside her waiting to break out on prom night I'd missed out on the experience of a lifetime. She was hot and she was damned near insatiable and she took me to my absolute limits. At six in the morning she was trying to get me to respond again and I just could not answer the call. We'd made love four times and I just didn't have a fifth in me.

"Maybe tonight," I told her, "but no way I can go again until I've had some rest."

"Tonight is out because it is my parent's twenty-fifth wedding anniversary and I have to be at their party, but I don't have anything going tomorrow."

I was just a touch slow in answering that and Harlina said, "It is too soon for me to be thinking of Toby's replacement Rob, but I would like to have someone around to help me get over him."

"My last class is at three."

"I get home from work at five."

"Six o'clock?"

"I'll be ready."

At two that Afternoon I got a call from Audrey.

"That was a rotten thing to say to Kyle and why were you following me anyway?"

"What's the matter Audrey? He didn't have a condom or did he have one and wouldn't take a chance? And I didn't follow you Audrey. Mike, Ben and I were there an hour before you got there and I sat there and watched you and your dickhead date for another hour before I stopped by to say hi. Think back on everything you did from the time you walked in the door until I stopped by your table and you will know what I saw. Should what I saw have made me happy Audrey? Goodbye."

The phone rang again almost immediately and I took it off the hook and left it off until I left to go to the movies two hours later.

The next day I was taking my lunch break at the student cafeteria when Audrey sat down at my table. I looked up at her and said in a slightly unfriendly tone:

"What do you want?"

"I want to know what the hell you thought you were doing the other night. I'm here because you can't hang up on me here and if you get up and walk away I'll just get up and walk with you. I'm not letting you tune me out."

"You would be better off tuning me out me out than hearing what I have to say."

"I can't refute it until you do."

"You can't refute it anyway. I saw what I saw and there is absolutely no excuse – none! – for a woman to behave that way with a man when she already has – make that had – a steady boyfriend. If you behaved that way in public there is no doubt in my mind about what you were going to do in private. When I stopped at your table and said what I said, I did it in the hope that it would ruin your evening because God knows you had already ruined mine."

"You honestly think I would have done that? You have that low of an opinion of me?"

"Actions speak for themselves Audrey. You did everything but fuck him while I sat back in the corner and watched. He played with your ass and your tits and he had his tongue so far down your throat that it probably touched the backside of your belly button. You made absolutely no attempt to shut him down. All you did was smile and I'll say it again, if you were doing that out in the open in public there is no doubt in my mind at all about what was going on in private."

"I swear to you Rob that nothing was going to happen. Okay, maybe I did go a little overboard, but we were having a good time and I was just going with the flow. I told Kyle ahead of time that I had a steady boyfriend and not to expect anything."

"He obviously didn't believe you or he wouldn't have been taking the liberties he took and your allowing those liberties pretty much told him that you didn't really mean what you said."

"God damn it Rob, nothing happened. Nothing was going to happen. After you left the table Kyle asked me if you were my boyfriend and when I said yes he told me I should get up and go after you. The only reason I didn't is because I was pissed at you because I thought you were following me. Please Rob, you have to believe me. Nothing happened and nothing was going to happen."

"I don't know Audrey. It seems to me that I'm only your boyfriend until Monica gives you a call and then I'm not until she doesn't need you. I don't think I want that kind of a relationship. Three times we have had a problem and all three times were because of Monica. I'm a realist Audrey. There is no way I can come between two people who have a fifteen year friendship. No way can I say Monica or me, your choice. I think it is best that we just call it quits and move on. Sorry Audrey, but that's the way I see it."

I got up and headed for my next class.

Over the next three weeks I saw Audrey almost every day at school, but we didn't talk. Over the same period I got together with Harlina seven or eight times as we worked on our friends with benefits relationship. Then two things happened within three hours of each other that changed things.

The first was Harlina bumping into me at the student book store and telling me that she and Toby were going to give things another try and asking me if I would please never let him find out about what we had done together. I promised silence and wished her good luck.

The second thing happened at the end of my last class of the day. I found Monica waiting for me in the hall outside of the classroom. She stepped up to me and said:

"What the hell is wrong with you? Why are you being such a dickhead toward Audrey? That girl is in love with you and you are treating her like shit."

"What? You are pretending that you don't know what went on?"

"I know what went on. Nothing! That's what went on. I was with her the whole time from the time we picked her up until we dropped her off and outside of some touchy-feely shit nothing happened. Okay so the girl had a drink or two too many and got a little loose, but Kyle knew she was spoken for and Tom and I weren't going to let anything happen."

"If everyone knew she was spoken for why the hell were you asking her to date another guy?"

"Because I didn't know until you kicked her to the curb how she really felt about you. To me you were just another guy she was dating. I didn't know you were special to her until we picked her up and she told Kyle that all she was going to be was company and why. At that point Tom and I appointed ourselves as her babysitter.

"We hit the Aladdin and had several drinks and waited for the band before we found out that their van got in an accident on the way to the lounge. We probably could have done with a few less drinks, but what the hell; we were out to have a good time. Nothing happened and nothing was going to happen. Kyle even told Aud to run after you after you left our table.

"The poor girl is a wreck. She comes to school and then goes home and sits and cries. If you have any feelings at all for her give the kid a break. You need to do something soon or you are liable to lose her. She is a lot tougher than she looks and sooner or later she will suck it up and move on. Think on it. Think on it hard."

She gave me a hard look and then she walked away.

I spent a day or two thinking about what Monica had said and it might have been true that nothing was going to happen. What it all came down to was that I had been hung up on Audrey since the ninth grade – over six years – and I missed not being with her.

When I got to the student union on Friday I saw Audrey sitting alone at a table and I took a deep breath, sucked it up and went over and sat down with her.

"I'm sorry Audrey. I overreacted and I apologize for the things I said."

"No need Rob. I've been over that night in my mind a dozen times and I can see why you thought what you thought. My behavior was inexcusable for someone who had a steady boyfriend."

I started to stand up and she asked, "Where are you going?"

"I just stopped by to apologize."

She pointed at the chair and said, "Sit! This is the first time you have talked to me in weeks and I want to keep it going. How have you been?"

We talked in general while we ate and just before I needed to leave for my next class Audrey asked:

"Do you have any plans for tonight?" and looked at me expectantly and just like that we were back together.

I proposed in October of our senior year, she said yes and we began making plans for a June wedding following graduation.

As it had been in the past we did double date with Monica and her beau from time to time. She had finally settled on Tom and for a change he wasn't a dick head like most of Monica's previous guys and I actually liked him.

On June sixteenth Audrey and I took our vows with Monica acting as her Maid of Honor and one month later Audrey stood with Monica as she and Tom were married.

The first six months of our marriage were trouble free and then there was another 'Monica Moment.' It was a Saturday night and Audrey and I had gone to dinner and after eating Audrey said she would like to go somewhere for a few drinks and some dancing so I drove us over to the Starlight Lounge. We had been there about forty-five minutes when Monica, Tom and two guys I didn't know arrived and took a table at the other end of the room from us. Naturally Audrey had to go over and say hi and I expected her to come back and tell me that we were going to move over to their table and join them.

That isn't what happened. Audrey was there for almost ten minutes and then she got up and danced with one of the guys I didn't know. After the dance she went back to Monica's table and two minutes later she got up and danced with the other guy I didn't know and after that dance she went back to Monica's table. I gave it another five minutes and then I got up and moved toward her. I was about halfway to her when she got up to dance with the first guy she had danced with. Was I pissed? Take a wild guess.

I got my wallet out and took out a twenty. I walked up to Audrey and the guy and grabbed Audrey's arm as I said:

"Excuse me for a second." I handed Audrey the twenty and said, "Here's cab fare." I turned and walked away.

I had the car started and was just taking it out of 'park' when the passenger door opened and Audrey got in. She slammed the door and said:

"What the hell is wrong with you Rob? You were actually going to leave me there?"

"Me? There is nothing wrong with me Audrey. It is all on you."

"What the hell do you mean by that?"

"Every time you get near Monica your brain short circuits. You went over to say hi to Monica and twenty-five minutes later, after dancing with two guys I've never seen before I'd finally had enough and I came over to tell you goodbye and leave you with who you obviously wanted to be with. It sure wasn't me. You forgot that I was even there."

"Get a grip Rob. All you ha…"

"Can it Audrey. I don't want to hear it."

"Damn it Ro…."

"Just shut the fuck up Audrey!!!"

The rest of the ride home was made in silence.

Things were cool around the house for the next three days and then on Tuesday Audrey woke me up with a blow job and when I was hard enough she moved over me and rode me cowgirl until we both came. She leaned forward and lay on my chest and said:

"I'm sorry baby."

I wisely didn't say a word.

Over the next couple of months I saw some things that disturbed me especially in the light of the time Audrey spent around Monica. One day as I was driving home from work I was passing the Motel 6 on Danbury and for some unknown reason I looked to my right just in time to see Monica come out of one of the rooms with a man who was most definitely not Tom.

Three weeks later I was having lunch with my boss at the downtown Hilton and I was sitting where I could see the lobby. I saw Monica come in with a man and they went to the check-in desk. Five minutes later they got into the elevator and I knew the Hilton well enough to know that there was nothing above the first floor but rooms.

I debated telling Audrey what I'd seen, but decided not to. She knew I didn't care for Monica and she would probably think I was trying to make something out of nothing. I didn't know Tom well enough to go to him and for all I knew he and Monica had one of those open marriage type things going.

Two months later Tom took a job at XYZ Industries out in California and I breathed a sigh of relief that Monica was gone from our life. And now here was Audrey telling me that Monica was back. Oh Joy!

***

Over the next month Audrey met Monica a half a dozen times for lunch and then came what I knew was coming.

"Honey if it is all right with you I'm going to stop after work tonight for drinks with Monica and a couple of girls that we grew up and went to school with. There are plenty of leftovers in the fridge so you can micro-wave yourself something for dinner okay?"

I was going to say no? Best friends for two-thirds of her life and I was going to say "I'd much rather you didn't" to her? I could just imagine what things would be like around the house if I did that. I didn't say a word, but I did give her a long look that told her that I had reservations based on previous experience and I hoped she would take those reservations to heart. Silly me. I should have told her exactly what I was thinking and taken the heat.

She was home by eight-thirty and told me she'd had a good time talking with her girlfriends and being brought up to date on the happenings in their lives. Then she took me to bed and did her level best to turn me into a total wreck. It was not our normal way. We usually made love three or four times a week, but normally it was some foreplay, some mutual oral, do it one time and then cuddle up and go to sleep. That night we went three times and Aud was doing her best to try and get me up for a fourth, but I just could not answer the call. As we lay there cuddling, I asked her what had gotten in to her.

"I wanted to show you how much I appreciate you." She was quiet for a moment and then said, "In talking to the girls tonight I came to realize that you are a treasure. Mary Sue has been married and divorced twice. Betsy is divorced and Carol is separated from her husband and it will probably end up in a divorce. Their husbands cheated on them, Mary Sue's first had a habit of coming home drunk and using her for a punching bag and there was a host of other faults that their ex-husbands had. I on the other hand seem to have the perfect husband so I thought I should do something to let you know how special you are."

I pulled her to me, kissed her and we fell asleep in each other's arms.

***

In the morning over breakfast Audrey told that the girls had such a good time that they were going to do it on a monthly basis. For the next two months, Audrey met with her friends on the third Thursday of the month and she was always home between eight and nine. During the same period she had lunch with Monica on the average of once a week. Then the monthly meetings turned into every two weeks or so, but Audrey was coming home between nine and ten and she always wanted to make love when she got there.

I started wondering when the get-togethers started taking place weekly and Audrey's time getting home went to between ten and eleven. The night she came home at ten forty-five was the night I finally decided that I needed to look into things.

The next Thursday I was parked down the street where I could see Audrey's car in the employee parking lot and when she got off work I followed her to the Gold Dust Lounge. I parked on the street so Audrey wouldn't see my car if she came out of the lounge for some reason. I gave her a half hour before I followed her in. I never wear a hat and I have 20/20 vision so my disguise was a windbreaker that I had bought that afternoon and that Audrey had never seen, a Cubs ball cap and a pair of horn-rimmed glasses with the lenses pushed out. And just for insurance I had on a fake mustache.

I walked in, saw Audrey at a table with five girls – one being Monica of course – and, I moved to a table on the other side of the room and settled in to watch. Until seven all that happened was that the girls sat and talked while nursing their drinks. At seven a band came in and set up and as soon as they started to play, guys started approaching the table and asking the girls to dance. Audrey said no to the first couple of guys, but after the band came back from their first break – and she'd had a few drinks – she got up and danced. Around nine one of the guys she danced with let his hands slip down to her ass and she didn't do anything about it.

Also around nine o'clock guys had joined every woman at the table except for Carol and Audrey. When the tune ended the guy who had put his hands on Audrey's ass walked her back to the table and she said something to him and he sat down and joined the group. About that time Carol picked up her purse and left. Audrey sat and talked with her guy and got up and danced with him two more times and both times he had his hands on her ass and was pulling her into him.

One by one the girls and the guys they had paired up with got up and left until only Monica, her guy and Audrey and the guy she had been dancing with were still at the table. That sat at the table and talked for maybe ten minutes and then the four of them got up and headed out of the lounge. I followed them out and saw Monica and her guy get in a car and drive off. Audrey and her guy got in his car and started to neck. I wanted to see what would happen so instead of storming over and breaking things up, I watched.

For twenty minutes they necked, talked and necked some more. Then I saw the man get a nasty look on his face as the dome light came on as the passenger door opened. I ran for my car and hurried home and got there just about ten minutes before Audrey showed up. She walked in and saw me and said:

"Oh good! You're up. I was afraid you would be asleep and I'm horny."

As we made love I was wondering who she was thinking of, me or the guy she had been with at the lounge.

***

The next Thursday I was again in place to watch and the scene was the same except for the cast of players. There were the same women, but the guys were all different. Audrey danced with a couple of different guys before one of them joined her at the table. The only thing different was that this time the guy didn't put his hands on her ass. The group broke up around ten and as happened the previous week Audrey ended up in her guy's car. They made out. I couldn't tell what their hands were doing, but their mouths stayed busy. When the dome light came on I saw an astonished look on the guys face just before I turned and ran for my car.

I again beat Audrey home by ten minutes and as she had been the previous week she was glad to see that I was still up to take care of the condition that her make out session had gotten her into. The third Thursday was a repeat of the first two. Audrey had never done anything but dance close and do some necking. At least she never did that I knew about, but I had no idea if she exchanged phone numbers and met any of them later.

Except for Thursdays she was always home a half hour after she got off work so if she was doing anything it was being done during her lunch breaks or maybe she was taking off from work during the day. I really doubted that she did either since she obviously could have left the bar earlier or have gone to meet someone right from work. I was not all that happy about what she was doing and I needed to let her know that and I decided to do it in a way that would get major attention.

***

Harlina had come to work where I worked and since we were old friends and one-time lovers we often had lunch together. I knew she was between boyfriends (her marriage to Toby had ended) so I asked her if she was up for doing me a big favor. I told her what was going on with Audrey and what I wanted to do. She laughed and told me to count her in.

The next Thursday I again followed Audrey to the Star Dust only this time I waited until she had parked her car and had gone inside. I pulled into the lot and parked just to the right of her and then I sat and waited. At seven-ten Harlina, who had gotten there before Audrey and had taken the table where I usually sat, called me and told me that Audrey was out on the dance floor.

Without a disguise this time, I walked in and walked directly over to Harlina's table and sat down with my back to the dance floor and asked Harlina if any of them had noticed me. She said it didn't look like anyone at the Audrey's table had. We sat and nursed our drinks while Harlina kept me up to date on what was going on behind me. Finally Audrey started dancing with the same guy and when he joined her at her table I put my plan into action.

The next time Audrey and her guy got up to dance Harlina and I got up and moved out onto the floor. I made sure that I kept turned so I wasn't looking at Audrey and let Harlina be my eyes.

"Okay, she has just seen you. Her face went a little pale. She just maneuvered her guy so her back is to you. I think she thinks you haven't seen her yet. She just said something to the guy and they are dancing back toward their table. She still has her back to us."

"We need to get out of here before she has a chance to get out first."

We went back to our table, Harlina got her purse and without looking at Audrey's table we left the lounge and went to my car. As soon as we were in the car Harlina slid over next to me and we pretended to be making out. Harlina was looking over my shoulder at the door to the bar and about two minutes after we got into the car, she said:

"She just came out. She's alone. She's scanning the parking lot. Uh-oh, she just spotted us and she looks pissed. She's walking to her car. She's in the car, but she is just sitting there watching." Harlina was silent for a couple of minutes and then she said, "She started the car. There she goes, she's out of the lot."

"Thanks sweetie. I owe you one."

"Keep me in mind lover. If things don't work out for you give me a call. As I remember it, we were pretty good together way back when."

She got out and went over to her car and I drove over to Denny's and had a burger and some fries. I went home at ten-thirty and Audrey was sitting on the couch when I got there.

"Oh good! You're up. I was afraid you would be asleep and I'm horny. Come on Aud, let's go to bed and have some fun."

"You bastard!! How could you do that to me?"

"Do what Aud?"

"I saw you with that tramp Harlina so don't you be asking me "what". You know damned well what you did."

"Was there something wrong with it?"

"You know damned well there is something wrong with it."

"Wait a sec here Aud, I need to see if I understand what is going on here. You go out every Thursday evening, dance with guys and then go out in the parking lot and make out with them in their cars and then come home and tell me that you are horny. At least that is the way it has been for the three weeks I followed you."

Her face lost all of its color.

"If it was good enough for you to do Audrey, it should be good enough for me too, don't you think? Come on Aud, let's go have some fun."

I got up and headed for the bedroom, but Audrey didn't follow. About fifteen minutes later I heard her come up the stairs and go into the spare bedroom so I rolled over and went to sleep.

***

When I got up in the morning I found Audrey sitting at the kitchen table drinking coffee. She didn't look like she'd had a good night. I poured myself a cup of coffee and was fixing myself a bowl of cereal when she said:

"Why were you following me?"

"Because you were with Monica and you have a history of being stupid when you are around her. When your night out with the girls went from one night a month to weekly and your come home times went from eight o'clock to ten-thirty I thought it was time that I check things out. It seems that I was right. Unfortunately even though I followed you I wasn't able to get answers to all of my questions."

"Questions?"

"Yeah Audrey, questions. Things like did you exchange phone numbers with the guys and then meet up with them later on your lunch breaks or take time off from work during the day to have a little afternoon recreational sex? Also, while watching I couldn't see anything below shoulder level so I couldn't see if you were giving the guy a hand job or if he was finger fucking you. I kind of suspect that they were since you always were so horny when you got home. I guess I'll need to put a private detective on you to find out about the lunch times and leaving work."

She was silent as I ate my cereal and then I went up showered and dressed for work. When I came out of the bedroom Audrey was still sitting at the table and when I took my car keys off of the hook on the side of the cupboard she said:

"What are you going to do?"

"That should be obvious Audrey. As long as you have your Thursday nights I'm going to have mine. See you tonight." I headed off to work.

Normally Audrey and I get off work close to the same time, but I usually get home first, but when I got home that night Audrey was home and dinner was ready to be put on the table. Knowing that I had the high ground I was a little on the sarcastic side with her.

"Have a good day Aud? Take a long lunch maybe?"

She gave me a nasty look and snapped. "No! I didn't even leave the building."

I shrugged and spooned some mashed potato onto my plate as I said, "Too bad I can't be sure of that. I haven't had time to get the private detective yet."

We ate the meal in silence and when we were done Audrey said, "I want to answer your questions."

"What questions?"

"The ones you asked this morning. I never gave anyone a phone number. I have never met anyone during my lunch periods and I have never taken off from work during the day to meet anyone. It doesn't matter that you couldn't see what was going on below shoulder level because nothing was going on down there. As for the question you didn't ask – what was I doing – I was being a bitch!"

"I didn't ask that question because I don't care why you were doing it. I have already come to accept that you become a brain dead zombie whenever you come within three feet of Monica."

"You might not want to know, but I'm going to tell you anyway. I said I was doing it because I was being a bitch. Every one of those guys saw my wedding rings and knew I was married, but they came after me anyway. I got a kick out of letting them buy me drinks and then leading them on until they thought they were home free. I went out to their cars with them, let them get all hot and bothered, and then I left them with a case of blue balls. Think about it Rob. Did you ever see the same guy twice come on to me? In fact, did you ever see one of the guys I did it with back at the bar the next week? No you didn't."

I remembered the look on the face of the first guy I'd seen her with when she got out of his car and the astonished look on the face of the last guy I watched her with when she left him.

"I told you why I was always horny when I came home to you. It is the God's honest truth Rob, you are a treasure and I was always glad to come home to you after being exposed to assholes."

I looked at her for maybe a minute and then said, "And how were you going to explain it to me when one of those guys you teased didn't take no for an answer and just took what he wanted? Did you expect that I would accept "I was just kidding Rob and it got out of hand"?"

She looked ashen and said, "I never thought about that."

"That's the problem Audrey. You never think when you are around Monica."

She was quiet for a bit and then said, "What now?"

"Simple Audrey, I said it last night. You do Thursdays; I do Thursdays."

"No Rob, I mean right now?"

"Right now?"

"I feel an obligation. You were horny last night and I didn't do anything about it. I don't know about you, but with me the horny's linger."

I smiled and said, "It's the same with me."

We left the dirty dishes on the table and headed for our bedroom. We were exhausted when we finished and as Audrey snuggled up to me she said:

"No more Thursdays baby, no more Thursdays." Seconds later there was the soft breathing of a sleeping woman.

***

A month went by and Audrey didn't go out on Thursdays and then one Wednesday morning my secretary buzzed me on the intercom and told me there was a Miss Torpin there to see me. It took me several seconds before I remembered that Torpin was Monica's maiden name. I told Jill to send her in.

I stood as Monica came in and I asked her to have a seat. She looked as hot and sexy as she always had and as she sat and crossed her magnificent legs I wondered, as I often had before, why I had never cottoned to her. She saw where I was looking and she smirked and then said:

"The Evil Bitch is here to ask you for a favor."

"Evil bitch?"

"Audrey and I have no secrets from each other. She has told me all about how you believe I cast some sort of spell over her whenever she is around me."

I just sat there and looked at her.

"I think the world of Audrey and I would never let anything happen to her that would cause her pain. I always have her best interests at heart. I know what she was doing on her nights out with the girls and I didn't interfere because I know Audrey, I know how she feels about you so I know that she would never do anything that would cost her your love. She belongs to you totally and I believe I told you that in a high school hallway once upon a time."

"What is this about Monica?"

"I want you to let Audrey out of jail."

"Out of jail? What the hell are you talking about?"

"The girls miss Audrey. She was part of our group, but she won't leave the house because of what you might think she was up to, because of what you think happens to her when she is near me. That girl would no more cheat on you than I could stay celibate for a week. Besides, if I thought she was leaving the bar to do you dirt I would grab her arm, pull her back and slap some sense into her. Unlike the rest of the girls in the group she has it made. She has what the rest of us want and she knows it."

"That's part of the problem Monica. The three weeks I followed her, you and all the others left the bar with a different man every night. You are setting an example."

"So what Rob? Every girl at that table except Audrey is single or in the process of getting single. They have no vows that need to be honored and looking for a life partner is part of the human condition. Two of them have met guys at that bar that they think they have a good chance of having a stable relationship with. I play the field because, to be absolutely honest about it, I have never found any one man who can handle me and my appetites. I have often thought that you might be the one, but alas, you belong to Audrey. Anyway, I'm asking you to let Audrey come join us on Thursdays. You don't have to worry about her Rob and deep down inside you know that. Think about it okay? Nice seeing you Rob. Take care." She got up and left.

I watched the sway of her ass as she walked out of my office and I was human enough to wonder if indeed I was the man who could handle her.

***

I spent most of the day and a good part of the evening thinking about Monica's visit. Audrey and I made mad, passionate love that night and afterwards as I lay there in the warm after glow, I admitted to myself that Monica was right. I loved Audrey and I knew that Audrey loved me and that she was mine. Part of love is trust.

In the morning over breakfast I casually asked Audrey what time she would be home that night and she said:

"The usual. Sometime between five-thirty and six."

"That won't even give you time for one drink."

"What are you talking about?"

"It is Thursday isn't it?"

She sat there and stared at me for almost thirty seconds while I sat there and waited for a reply. Finally she said:

"Are you sure?"

"You are a big girl now. You know how to handle yourself."

She got up and came over and sat down on my lap. She kissed me and asked:

"Got time for a quickie before going to work?"

I did.

=The End=

Here is a sample from another story you may enjoy!

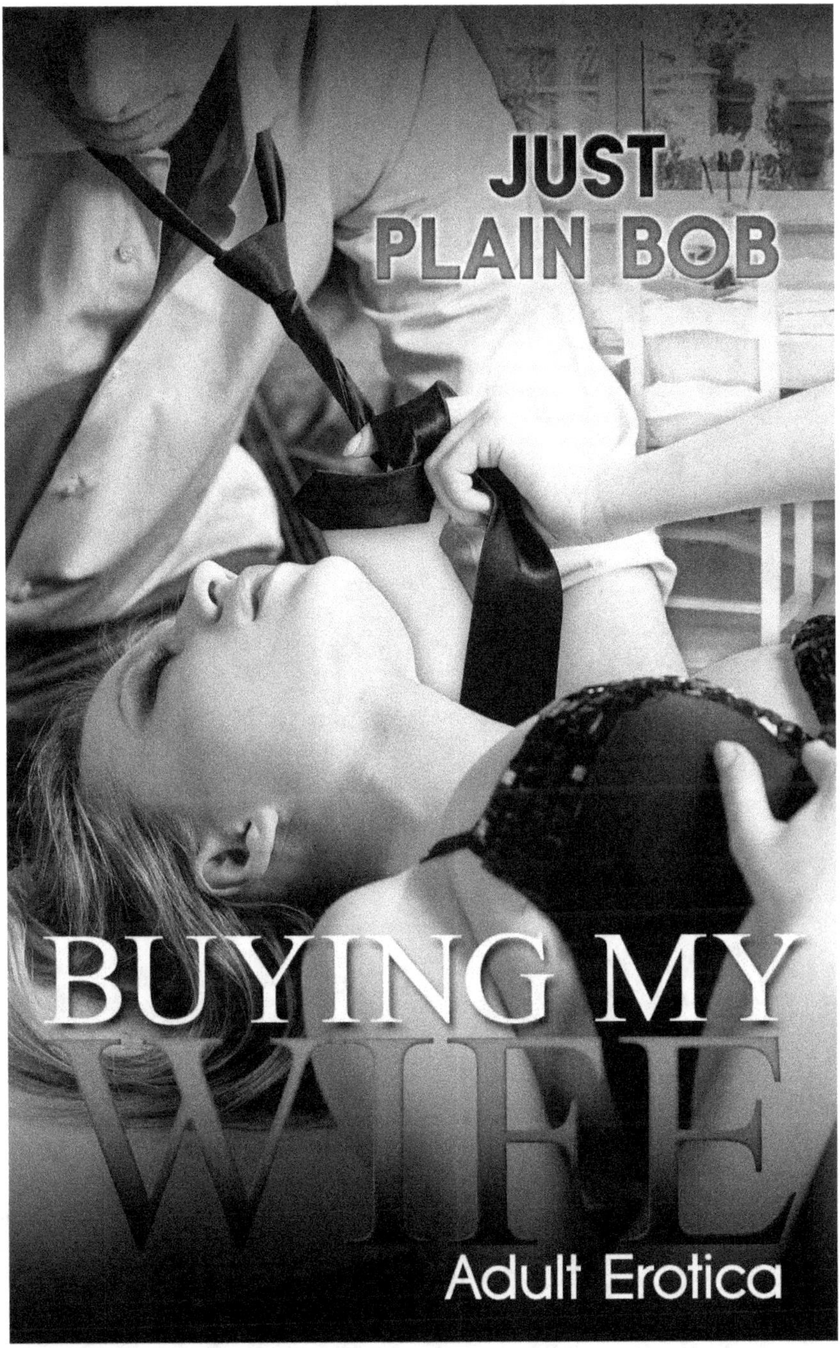
JUST
PLAIN BOB
BUYING MY
WIFE
Adult Erotica

The first thing I did when I got back to my office was get out the Yellow Pages and turn to Investigators and Investigative Services. There were three within two blocks of my office and the first two I called couldn't see me for three or four days but the third one said, "Come on down." As I walked the two blocks to Acme Investigative Services I tried to think of what Hargrove must have been smoking. There was no way that Abby could be having an affair with him let alone be planning on marrying him. We were too happy together. We had a great relationship, but at the same time I couldn't help but feel that something made Hargrove approach me and the best way to find out what it was was to put someone on the case to check things out. Maybe Abby was just a good friend and he misunderstood her feelings. For my own peace of mind I needed to find out what was going on.

I met with Mr. Owen Paulson and filled him in on my meeting with Hargrove. I told him that I seriously doubted that my wife was being unfaithful, but I did need to know what Hargrove was up to. The only times Abby was out of the house were for her Tuesday night book club and discussion group, her Thursday night bridge club meeting and her Saturday morning beauty shop appointment to have her hair done while I played golf with three of my friends. I gave Paulson all the information he asked for regarding Abby and then I gave him a check to get him started. Since it was a Wednesday he told me they would put an operative on Abby Thursday morning when she left the house to go to work and then watch her until the following Tuesday. He told me I could stop by or call him Wednesday for a report.

As I walked back to my office I spent more time trying to figure out what Hargrove was really after. I had absolutely no doubt about Abby's love for me, but I could not figure out for the life of me what Hargrove's angle was.

Abby usually beat me home and when I got home that night she was in the kitchen fixing dinner. She stopped what she was doing, came to me and put her arms around me and kissed me. Dinner and dishes out of the way we curled up on the couch to watch some TV and Abby moved in next to me, put her head on my shoulder and cuddled up next to me. This woman cheating on me? No way!

If you enjoyed this sample then look for **Buying My Wife**.

Also by this Author:

The Prodigal Family: The Abbotts

Watching My Shared Wife

The Waitress and the Runaway Husband

Baiting Mr. Little

Too Hot for Henry

Chuck's Fantasy

The Redhead's Desires

Rescued at Riley's

His Every Fantasy

Open Mike Night

Pursuit for Revenge

Why Does He Do That?

Halloween & Drugs

Tracey

When Rob Met Kari

Becoming a Shared Wife, Vol. 1 –
(Wife Sharing and Other Adventures)

Becoming a Shared Wife, Vol. 2 –
(Hazardous Wives)

Becoming a Shared Wife, Vol. 3 –
(Wives Who Stray)

Her Illicit Adventures

What I Want To Do To Her

Too Fun To Give Up

Creamed

Stepping Out

Hottest Wife

Naughty Wives

Deepest and Darkest

More Than She Can Take

Jennifer's Toes

The More The Sexier

Spice Up

Cyndi

Naughty And Nice

House Of Lovers

Hungry For More

Sweet Revenge

Turning Mommies Wild: The Carriage Tales

Bought And Used

Get Me Off

The Gambler

Gail's Price

You may also like the books by these authors:

Gideon Elliot

The Good Bitch

Surprising Erotic Discovery

BDSM Erotica

She knew that if she wasn't there when he got back from the garage, he didn't like it.

"I'm an old-fashioned kinda guy," he explained one night after he'd smacked her around because dinner wasn't ready when he got home and the house was a mess. He'd had a long and hard day, and sometimes a guy loses his temper. He wouldn't be normal if he didn't.

"I mean, I work all day to support us, and all you gotta do, I mean all you gotta do is keep up your end of the bargain, right? I mean that's what you wanted, wasn't it? Just when I come home, my slippers are out and there's a hot meal ready, and the house is a place I can be proud to say I live in. And if you fix yourself up a little, try to look a little pretty, hey, that's icing on the cake. You know what I'm sayin'?"

"I do, Larry; you're right. I'm sorry."

"I know you are," he said, taking her in his arms. "What am I gonna do with you?"

"I'll get better, Larry. I mean it. I want to."

She was looking up at him, now, wishing he would kiss her, and he did. A frisson of electricity passed through her and her body fell limp against his.

"That's it, baby. Papa's home," he said and he slid his hand down her back beneath her cutaway jeans and started circling and teasing her budding aureole and then plunged in. She gasped. Her eyes glazed over.

* * *

He threw her onto the bed spread eagle, face down, and pinned her there with the might of his arms and knees.

"Tell me what you want me to do."

"I want you to fuck me."

"Tell me where."

"In my pussy."

"Where?"

"Up my pussy."

He circled her wrists with his fists and pulled her arms back. She felt as if her shoulder blades were cracking.

"Where?"

"Up my pussy," she repeated beginning to whimper.

He pulled her arms more. She began to sob.

"Where do you want me to fuck you, bitch?"

"In my pussy," she cried.

"Where?"

 The pain was becoming excruciating.

"Up my ass."

"Again."

"Up my ass."

"Because I'm a pig."

"Ask for it, pig."

"Please fuck me up the ass."

"Beg."

The pain was intense.

"Please, Larry."

"Please what?"

"Please fuck me?"

"Where?"

"Please fuck my ass. Oh, please fuck my ass. Fuck my ass."

His cock was like a dagger poking at her now, and his breathing was wet with spittle on her neck as he tore into her flesh with his teeth.

"Tell me why."

"Because I'm a shitty, worthless little bitch and need to get fucked up the ass."

He ploughed into her. She screamed until the pain crashed like lightning, and then everything caught and turned upside down as in an inverting mirror and the pain turned to an ecstasy of pleasure she had forgotten, and she screamed as he stabbed her repeatedly, fucking her ass and digging his fingers into her arm pits and grabbing her breasts in fistfuls and scratching her nipples with his calloused finger tips until he collapsed on top of her and she almost couldn't breathe.

"You're gonna feel that all day tomorrow," he crowed, "and you're gonna know for sure whose bitch you are."

If you enjoyed this sample then look for **The Good Bitch** **by Gideon Elliot.**

R.W. Pell

Escape to Kingdom Cum

Erotic Romance and Submission

She glanced at the customer, noticing only that he was male and his shopping was for one. He was unremarkable she processed his goods through the scanner and packed them into a carrier bag as she went. Took his money and offered the change. She would have instantly gone on to the next customer, but a rich vibrato voice informed her she had made a mistake and the hand that belonged to the voice was trying to return some coins that she had given. Mary began to fluster as she always did in these circumstances and in her panic, couldn't find the key to open the cash drawer.

Eventually, she fought for control of her senses and thanked him for his honesty while shutting the errant drawer. That was it really. Mary sat at the till for the rest of the day. Her unflattering light blue uniform covering her, with her hair savagely pulled back in a tight bun, unremarkable in her self and mostly unnoticeable to any observer.

Mary had taken to allowing herself the luxury of a cafe latte on her way home. It was perhaps, the only luxury she did have. Her usual table was empty and her conversation with the serving girl was restricted to her request for the foamy beverage. Mary revelled in her private thoughts and was oblivious of the rest of the world as it went about its business.

"Mind if I join you." There was something familiar about the rich tenor of the voice, but Mary merely nodded her consent and didn't look up.

"Looks like rain again," he remarked casually. "I don't know when summer is going to start, do you?"

Mary looked up at the direct question and shook her head. She had never learned the niceties of conversation and preferred to stay quiet.

"Ah! I almost didn't recognise you. You're the girl at the checkout, aren't you?" His smile creased his eyes and deepened the azure quality of the blue.

Mary blushed furiously, remembering him now and then associating him with her error.

"I…I'm sorry for the mistake." Her tremulous voice was barely audible over the hubbub of the coffee shop and nervously, she wrung her hands in her lap below the level of the table and beyond his sight. Her own eyes remained downcast and she wished that the floor would open up and swallow her, whole.

"Ah! No worries," he said easily. "We all make them, don't we?"

She caught the movement of his hands as he used them to emphasise his words. She flinched, thinking he was about to strike her, he noticed the involuntary spasm and dropped his hands so they lay flat on the table, he consciously kept them there.

"I didn't get your name."

"Mary."

"Well hello, Mary, it is a pleasure to meet you."

She looked up sharply to see if he was making fun of her with condescension, but she met a pair of smiling eyes that, although creased with a smile, were not cruel in anyway. Her flush of anxiety was becoming one of something else and she started to fluster again.

"Where does Mary come from I wonder?" His question could have been taken in a mocking sense, but his smile told otherwise. "And I wonder what Mary is like away from the Supermarket?"

"I'm sure I don't know," she answered and then continued, "I have to go now."

"Ah! Now that is a shame so it is. Wouldn't you stay for another and keep a lone man company?" He indicated her half empty coffee cup as he asked the question.

Mary was mortified. Her total experience of men talking to her was her father, usually angry; her husband, also angry and usually drunk; her priest and the doctor, but him, only when she absolutely had to go. The Manager at the supermarket rarely said more than one or two words and that was it for verbal contact with the male of the species. She rushed from the table, colliding with the next in her haste to get away and leaving behind, a carrier bag with that night's dinner and a bemused man who wondered what on earth had gotten into the woman.

That night, as she lay in her bed, covered from head to toe in a flannelette nightgown and blankets pulled up to her chin, Mary dreamed. She dreamed of this stranger and in a completely naïve innocence, dreamt of his holding her in his arms, warm and protective. Sex was not part of her subconscious. It was an event that had happened on a few occasions when Tom stank of Guinness or whiskey. It had resulted in her lovely daughter and the removal of her ability to have children. Sex had never been a joyous explosion of feelings and nerve jangling climaxes. Sex was a sordid and shameful subject, only to be done to create a child. That was why Tom was right to leave. She couldn't give him children. It was all her fault.

"Hail Mary Mother of god..." Even in her sleep, Mary was completely subjugate to her religion and fervently believed herself to be the most loathsome woman ever to have disgraced his garden.

But, a seed of doubt had been sown. Someone had taken enough interest in her to talk and make an acquaintance.

They saw each other once or twice over the next few days. He bought her a coffee and she returned the compliment the very next time, not wanting to be beholding to anyone. Their conversation was more than a little stinted. Mary couldn't find the ways to articulate, unused to describing herself or her life, believing them to be uninteresting. She would rather have sat there, listening to him tell her of his travels around the world as a sailor in the Merchant Navy. Whole vistas of unimaginable scenes flowed around her mind as his narrative enticed and lured her out of her mundane and urban life to the tropics and the Far East.

Mary found herself looking critically in her bedroom mirror and realised that she was nothing at all to look at. Her clothing, although clean, was not fashionable in any century she knew of. She threw her blouse, skirt and underwear to the floor in disgust and then, hesitantly, looked critically at her naked body for the first time in her life.

Looking back at her was a slightly built woman, obviously approaching her forties, but had not been ruined by constant childbirth. Her hair, always a constant source of annoyance, was still pulled back and tightly wound into her normal bun. Mary pulled the pins and allowed her hair to cascade; pleased with the way it fell to below her shoulder blades and waved in natural curves. The mousy colour had deepened into a chestnut that had a rich lustre about it. She could hardly believe that it was her hair and was amazed at its length and vibrancy of colour. The only time it was unwound was when she washed it. Then, while wet, it appeared to be black and lank.

She skipped her face, not wanting to be too critical in her appraisal and looked at her breasts, noticing for the first time in her life, that the left one was slightly smaller than the right, but not too noticeably. Her bra size had remained the same since her wedding, 34 B cup. It was a good size she thought.

Her stomach was still quite firm and flat. You had to really look hard to see any stretch marks. She noticed a dark brown mole on her left hip and wondered when that had happened.

Mary's pubic area had a lush growth of hair, darker than her head that formed an almost perfect triangle, with slightly curved sides. She spent little time admiring that part of her body, but travelled to her legs. They were good legs by anyone's reckoning. The skin was flawless and almost transparent in whiteness. Her musculature was clearly visible beneath the taut covering. Only a few hairs grew below her knee. Mary hated her feet. It was one of those irrational hatreds women have of their anatomy. With Mary, it was her feet. Apart from her hands, her feet were the only part of her body she had studied at any time.

All in all though, not a bad package she thought. She turned this way and that, trying to see what her behind looked like and marvelled in the swish of her hair as she turned and twisted.

Then Mary asked the reflection looking back at her. Why am I standing here admiring myself? What am I looking at? She didn't know the answer to either question and in her naivety, she was not aware that she was in preparation for a sexual encounter and was merely checking out the validity of what she was offering.

She looked at her legs again, remembering the only time she had worn a short skirt. She had only got to the foot of the stairs when her father screamed at her and tore the clothes from her back, repeating over and over as he beat her. Ye harlot ye, I'll learn yeah, ye harlot and Jezebel. It took Mary several years more to find out what a harlot was and who Jezebel was supposed to be. That was one thing she never forgave her father for. The beatings she thought she deserved, but never to be called anything like that.

Mary dressed in her usual black or dark brown shapeless dress and cinched it together with a plastic belt effectively hiding any allure she might have had. But, she left her hair down.

A few days later, she met him again. Her confidence grew in exponential increments with every encounter. She was still to talk about herself and still did not know his name.

"Mary…" He had a way of saying her name that made it sound like the most beautiful word in the language. "Mary, I have sat here and told you all about me and not once have I asked you anything about you. Are you married? Where do you live? Do you have brothers, sisters anything or anything and everything?"

"You might have told me so much about you, but you never have told me your name."

"Oh Bejayzus!" He threw his hands up and almost fell over backwards off the stools they were sitting on. Mary smiled at his actions and blushed at his profanity of the Lord's name.

"So I haven't. It's Michael, Michael Donnelly and very pleased it is to be meeting with yeah." He lapsed into an Irish drogue that sounded peculiar from an Irishman and had Mary laughing fit to bust before she realised the spectacle she was making of herself and quickly brought herself under control.

"Ah Mary, Mary, that is a grand smile you be having there, 'tis a shame to be hiding it." His eyes danced in merriment and Mary felt her heart lurch.

Somehow, they sat there for an hour while she told him of her life to this point. He listened and made no comments while she spoke, just the occasional shake of his head, as if in disbelief. Mary talked and talked until she realised the time.

"Oh Mercy!" She wailed through her fingers as they covered her mouth in shock. Eileen will be after killing me or ringing the hospitals. I have to go home. She jumped up, spilling an empty coffee cup as her thigh caught the edge of the table. She grabbed her bags and was on the point of flight.

"I'll drive you," he said it simply, but in a voice that was not about to take no for an answer.

"I...I couldn't," she protested weakly, but it was already settled as he relieved her of her bags and guided her to the exit and his car waiting in the parking zone.

She directed him and observed the casual ease with which he negotiated the evening traffic. She also took the opportunity to appraise his form, features and body.

She guessed him to be a few years older than her. His years at sea had ingrained lines into his face, but wasn't detrimental to the whole aspect. His black hair was swept back off his forehead was in need of cutting and flicked up at the nape of his neck.

His open necked sport shirt showed his torso to be quite well built, certainly not 'He Man', but well proportioned and powerful. His slacks gave nothing away, but were neatly pressed and clean. Mary liked his teeth. They had a pure whiteness to them and uniformity rarely seen. She also liked his mouth. The expressive quirks and full lips did things to her imagination.

Mary noticed her curtains twitch as she and Michael ascended the stone stairs to her front door. He carried the bags and then left her with a cheery wave and a private smile that passed between them.

Eileen fairly gushed as her mother shut the door in an obvious reflective state of mind. Demanding to know who the Hunk, as she put it, was and where did she know him from. Mary fended off the inquisition and prepared dinner in a distracted vortex of mangled thought.

She found herself preening, something she had never done before, but there she was, in front of the mirror, preening and primping her hair.

They continued to meet at the coffee shop. Daily, easily chatting and talking, getting to know each other until, one particular, memorable Friday. This Friday was different because Michael asked her out.

"Perhaps we could go to the pictures, dancing or how about a meal?" He asked; Mary accepted without hesitation, but then, immediately after her acceptance, the doubts crowded in.

What would she wear? How did you go on a date? She began to panic again and left hurriedly to the safe domain of the flat. Eileen proved to be invaluable, calming and then knowledgeable. Secretly, she was thrilled for her mother and pulled out all the stops. Although Mary couldn't really afford it, they went clothes shopping, a first of many firsts to come. Mary ceded to Eileen's dress sense and at the end of the wearying excursion, had to admit that her purchases looked fantastic on her.

Just before the appointed time of Michael picking her up, Mary cast an appreciative glance and a twirl over her ensemble. She would never in her life, have picked out pastel colours, but had to agree that the subtle shades and fineness of the materials accentuated her figure and highlighted her hair. Another first was the introduction of makeup. Mary had never once worn anything on her face apart from a bruise. Eileen once again, worked a magic that even Mary had to admit, looked absolutely perfect.

Michael arrived punctually and waited in the living room while Mary touched up and preened with Eileen in attendance. Then, together they entered the living room and faced Him, One young girl presenting her prodigy for inspection, the other a middle-aged woman who was feeling very young and more nervous than she had ever been in her life. This was it, a first step on a path that she could have no idea of its destination.

Michael smiled that winning smile that lit his eyes as he turned from the mantelpiece.

"OH! I must be in the wrong house, I thought Mary lived here, but I must be wrong." His teasing pleased Eileen and produced a playful punch from her to his arm.

"Mary, you look stunning." The simplicity of his comment and the sincerity with which it was delivered went straight to her heart. If she wasn't in love before, with this man, then she was now and she liked the feeling. "Shall we go?" He offered his arm and they left to go to the movies.

Mary couldn't remember the film, the actors or the plot, so wrapped in the attentions of Michael was she, that any peripheral stimulation was ignored. The film finished and they filed out into the cool night air. It must have rained, but she didn't notice. They had a drink in a local bar and then decided to go home to Mary's flat for a coffee.

They climbed the stone steps and Mary fished around in her purse for the keys. Eventually, she found them and began to unlock the door. Michael grasped her lightly, but firmly enough to turn her around to face him. Instinctively, she lifted her eyes to see what he intended and realised that he was going to kiss her.

It was a tender brush of lips, the first act of passion she had ever had and a moment that burned into her memory for always.

"I have wanted to do that for a long time, Mary," Michael breathed into her ear as he gently held her in his arms. Then he kissed her again, parting his lips, Mary responded and felt his tongue run across her teeth. Her knees very nearly gave way as her heart raced and thumped in her breast.

She had to break it off in case she feinted and turned to open the door.

"Goodnight, Mary. Thank you for the evening." He was turning to go, but Mary almost squeaked her plea for him to come in for the promised coffee.

She put the kettle on the gas ring and scooted Eileen out, who was lurking in the kitchen, eager to hear all that had happened on the night out. Tactfully, she withdrew to her bedroom when she learned that Michael was sitting in the front room.

After the coffee, they sat silently side by side on the settee, contemplating what was next. They had shared a first kiss, for Mary, her first real kiss. She didn't know what came next because sex had only been for the procreation of children or the gratification of her husband.

Michael took her hand in his and twisted towards her. He could see the confusion running across her face like print on a page. She looked like a stricken mouse at the mercy of a cat.

"Mary, I would love to make love to you, but, knowing what has gone before, would prefer to wait, if that is what you want. I think you are an absolutely fantastic woman, so beautiful and I am falling in love with you and don't want to spoil anything between us."

If you enjoyed this sample then look for **Escape To Kingdom Cum** by **R.W. Pell**

HOT EROTICA

HIRED FOR
Their Pleasure
A LATE BLOOMER'S 1ST TIME

JACK RYDER

"Mom was right, you have a gorgeous body," her voice startled me awake. I guess I must have stirred a bit when my body felt the pressure of someone sitting down on the bed next to me. I was still a bit groggy as I open my eyes to see Katie sitting there staring down at me. It took a few moments for to remember that I was completely naked. I instinctively reached to pull the blankets up but found that they had been kicked off onto the floor at some point in my sleep.

"Should I lock the door from now on, or is it acceptable for me to be naked every time you barge into my house unannounced?" My voice was hoarse and strained. I could see a look of lust on her face as she gawked at my flaccid prick. "You can be naked any time I come over," she told me with her eyes never leaving my dick. "Besides, Mom told you I would be over for breakfast." I glanced at the clock and it was ten after 9am.

"Do you think I'm pretty, Jake?" She whispered. "Oh hell yes, Katie...you are so very sexy," I told her as I felt a slight wiggle. Kathleen was wearing that tiny white bikini again. The way she was seated with one leg dangling off the bed and the other leg bent beside her, left her legs spread wide apart and I could see her pussy lips pressed tight against the crotch of her bottoms.

"But, I'm so skinny and I have no tits," she complained softly. "Even Stevie has bigger tits than I have," she lamented. "Are you kidding me?" I chuckled. "With that sexy slender body, those perky cone shaped tits are perfect." I gasped. "There are many men that prefer perky tits rather than the big globe type," I informed her. "You are incredibly sexy just the way you are, sweetie."

"Do you think you could like these as much as my mother's?" Katie reached up and untied her top so it fell forward to expose her breasts to me. "Ooooh Katie, look at you," I gasped as she reached back to undo the other string and her top fell off. Her small 32A cone shaped tits were less than a foot from my face. Her pink puffy nipples were exactly the same as her mother's but seemed more pronounced since her tits are more cone shaped. She also had those pure white triangles from her bikini tan line that has always aroused me deeply. "Damn, those are sexy," I gasped.

My dick had become fully rigid within seconds as I gazed at her exposed tits. "I see you're telling the truth," she giggled as she watched my dick bouncing against my belly. "You can touch them if you like," she whispered as she scooted a little closer and pulled her other leg up onto the bed. My hands were trembling noticeably as I reached forward to fondle both of her nubile little tits.

"That feels wonderful, Jake," she purred softly as she arched her back to press her breast firmly into my hands. I let go of her left breast and used placed my right hand around her waist so I could pull her forward. "Yes Jake, Yessssss," she moaned as I wrapped my lips around her left puffy pink nipple and began to gently suck on it.

I felt her moving slightly and then felt her right hand wrapping around my rigid prick. "It's so big," she cooed when she saw that she could barely get her hand all the way around my girth. "Oooh, God Yes," I moaned as she started to gently stroke up and down my shaft. "So good, Jake, it feels s-o-o-o-o good," she gasped when I moved my mouth to suck on her other nipple.

My legs were quivering on the bed as she slowly jerked me off while I feasted on both of her perky tits. "I was so hard for you yesterday," I confessed as she got me closer and closer to orgasm. "You made my meat so wet when you were modeling those clothes," she answered me with a moan.

If you enjoyed this sample then look for <u>Hired For Their Pleasure</u> by Jack Ryder.

John Rutter approached his front door very weary from his day's work. A last-minute meeting had pushed his day into overtime and at 8pm he was just getting home. As he entered, he was surprised to hear voices from within as he set his briefcase down. Walking into the living room, he was even more surprised to see his boss, Horace Ender, and his wife, Emma, along with the ubiquitous presence of Horace's bodyguard/right-hand man, Jared, all 6'8" and 275 pounds of sculpted black imperviousness. Even more jarring was the presence of Horace's secretary, Melissa, a 5'4" red-headed pixie with an upturned, freckled nose beneath bright green eyes.

"So, you're finally home," Jean, John's wife said, pressing her body into his and kissing him lightly on the lips. "Busy day?" she asked, her bright green eyes staring into his as her braless breasts rubbed lightly against his chest, her waist-length blonde hair swaying back and forth.

"Very," John replied, still wondering how he could have forgotten that everyone was coming over this evening.

"Sorry to surprise you, John," Horace said, at 65 still a silver-haired, energetic powerhouse of a man whose 6'3" frame was dwarfed by the presence of Jared standing behind him.

"Not at all," John replied, nonplussed. "I thought I had forgotten you were coming or something."

"Hello, John," Emma said, her silvery-grey hair tied back in a ponytail just like her husband's. At 63 and 5'6", Emma Ender was still a beautiful, willowy woman with bright blue eyes. "Nice to see you again."

"Emma," John replied, taking her hand and kissing her on both cheeks. "My pleasure. You look great," he said, admiring her and her husband, both very tanned from spending so much time at their home in Hawaii. "To what do we owe the pleasure?" he asked.

"Your future, John," Horace replied, a firm look on his face.

"My future?" John said a bit nervously.

"Yes," Horace answered. "Why don't you sit down and we'll talk," he said, indicating the large seat next to him.

As John settled nervously into the seat, everyone else settled down, too, Jean sitting between Melissa and Emma on the sofa while Jared stood behind John imposingly.

"Now see here, John," Horace began. "As far as your work goes, I can't say we've ever had a better, more productive employee, so rest assured on that score."

"I'm happy to hear it," John replied.

"Your energy, innovative thinking, and enthusiasm have all combined to bring in much business," Horace said. "So naturally we think of promoting you. We like to keep the best and the brightest and most promising at all costs."

"Wow, I don't know what to say," John said, truly surprised that this moment had come after only 2 years with the company.

"But we also consider other factors," Horace continued, "in deciding which people are worth keeping, factors such as honesty, morality, and suitability to our particular type of corporate culture. Being a productive worker just isn't enough anymore in today's marketplace."

"I understand," John replied.

"We're interested in determining whether you're such a person," Horace said. "But we do have some reservations, I must admit, which is why we're here tonight."

"What do you mean?" John asked, struggling to keep the nervousness from his voice.

"Well, we like to know that managers in our company are honest, truthful, and can be relied upon at all times, as well as whether they fit into our particular corporate culture," Horace said. "Are you such a person, John? Are you honest and truthful? Do you fully fit into our particular type of corporate culture? Can you be relied upon at all times to do what is required of you and do so with the utmost in discretion? Now, think before you answer. This is extremely important. Everything about your future with the company depends upon how you respond this evening."

Everyone just watched John expectantly, saying nothing. The tension was so thick you could cut it with a knife.

"The best answer I can give you," John replied after due consideration, "is that I always try to be honest and truthful. I'm not a saint and I don't always succeed, but it's important to me, too, so I try. As for being reliable and acting with discretion as far as the company is concerned, 150%," he stated. "I have to say that I've never had a job that was as challenging, yet as exciting and fun. I look forward to going to work each and every day."

"Yes, that we're well aware of," Horace said somewhat cryptically. "But we're referring to your entire life when we talk about honesty and truthfulness and integrity, and even to an extent our particular corporate culture. Was your answer only about work or did it also cover your life in general?"

"My life, period," John answered without hesitation.

"I see," Horace said, a disturbed look on his face.

"John, when we got married, we agreed to always be open and honest with each other, to share our lives completely," Jean said from her seat on the sofa. "No matter what."

"That's right," John agreed, nodding his head warily.

"Neither of us were virgins when we met, but I've been absolutely faithful to you ever since we got married," she continued.

"Can you say the same, John?" Emma asked quietly from the sofa. John just stared at the three of them sitting there, realizing suddenly that both Melissa and Emma were each holding one of Jean's hands.

"No," John replied quietly after a minute. "I can't say the same."

"I'm glad you're being honest with us, John," Horace said after a few moments of pregnant silence filled the room. "That's very important, believe me. Now, you're saying you've been unfaithful to your wife; is that correct?"

"Yes," John replied, hardly daring to look Jean in the face but not daring to look anywhere else.

"Has it been one woman, many women?" Horace asked.

"Just one," John answered.

"I see," Horace said, nodding his head. "And was this a one-time thing or an ongoing thing?"

"It's been ongoing," John admitted, hating the look of pain in Jean's eyes as she stared at him, white-knuckled as she held Melissa & Emma's hands.

"Are you in love with this other woman?" Horace asked.

"No," John answered, exhaling a huge breath. "It's just sex, lust."
"Your wife doesn't please you, satisfy you sexually enough?" Emma asked softly.

"Oh, no, it has nothing at all to do with Jean," John exclaimed. "I'm totally, 100% committed to her. I love her. Our sex life is good, great.

I never leave the house without..." he said, then stopped as he realized he was saying too much.

"Without what?" Emma asked, a smile almost creasing her face.

"Without, without..." John tried to say.

"Without fucking me," Jean filled in. "And when he gets home, that's usually the first thing that happens, we fuck. That's why I don't understand..."

"And if saving your marriage and your job, depended upon you stopping this behavior immediately, would you? Could you?" Horace asked.

"Yes," John replied emphatically. "My marriage and job are far more important to me."

"And you'd be willing to atone for your transgressions if need be?" Horace asked.

"Yes, if that's what's necessary," John said, nodding his head, feeling the sweat on his brow even though it was a cool evening and the windows were open.

"How shall you atone?" Horace asked almost rhetorically. "Is it possible to atone for this?" he asked, reaching down and picking up the remote control and pointing it at the television and pushing a button.

John stared in astonishment as a side-by-side picture of his office appeared on the television, one view being from the door, the other from the wall behind his desk facing the door. No part of his office was hidden from view.

"Shall we get started," John's voice came from the television, followed almost immediately by John himself with Melissa trailing…

If you enjoyed this sample then look for **Affairs, Conundrum, Atonement** by **George X. Bush.**

4FUN PUBLISHING
30 BOOK BOX SET
WET Bundle
MEGA COLLECTION OF SEX STORIES

"I've been constantly horny since my birthday and so I'm always wet and ready for you."

– The Biggest She's Ever Had, Just Plain Bob

Who wants to get wet?

This compilation of 30 books from 14 authors will surely get one hot and creamy.

One **green-eyed Lucy** takes a slave while a bombshell goes to the adult theater to indulge in some spanking. If that's not enough, there's a sex-change drama that can only make one wetter by **accepting her true pleasure**.

The women in this compilation are also getting so hot like the white chick craving for some black organ, which may just be **the biggest she's ever had**. Then there's the seductive **Mrs. Moon** who's just "craving for his touch."

The men are not to be outdone. There's **the Jason look-alike tradesman** or the priest that takes one to **the scene of sin** or that who gives the **playful foreplay**.

Every story gives reader a wet spot and by the end of this book, one is guaranteed to be inundated with eroticism.

Prepare to get wet with these stories:
Green-Eyed Lucy by George X. Bush
Bombshell by Matt Brooks
X-Virus by Lisa James
White Slut for Black by Sammy West
The Biggest She's Ever Had by Just Plain Bob

Mrs. Moon by Ben E. Dorm
The Tradesman by Ben E. Dorm
Brie's Diary by Samantha Tessen
The Scene of Sin Samantha Tessen
Bareback Romance by Ruby Reed
Everything I Wanted to Do by Scout Allen
Helen's First by R.W. Pell
Craving for his Touch by RW Pell
Pampered Wife by Jennifer Mueler
Private Response by Jennifer Mueler
Downtown and Out by Leo Pekon
Making the First Move by Leo Pekon
Nice and Slow by Uther Pendragon
Castle Nursery by Uther Pendragon
Playful Foreplay by Uther Pendragon
A Hero's Farewell by Uther Pendragon
After Break Special by Uther Pendragon
Feels Like the First Time by Uther Pendragon
One Hell of a Weekend by Mason Hess
One Night Stand by Mason Hess
Claiming Her Property by Mason Hess
Losing Control by Mason Hess
Rough Use by Mason Hess
Crossing The Limits by Mason Hess
Accepting Her True Pleasure by Mason Hess

If you enjoyed this sample then look for **WET Bundle** by **4Fun Publishing.**

www.ingramcontent.com/pod-product-compliance
Lightning Source LLC
Chambersburg PA
CBHW071416170626
46811CB00003B/1423